The Laureate's Party

The Laureate's Party →

A Red Fox Book

Published by Random House Children's Books
20 Vauxhall Bridge Road, London, SW1V 2SA

A division of The Random House Group Ltd
London Melbourne Sydney Auckland
Johannesburg and agencies throughout the world

1 3 5 7 9 10 8 6 4 2
First Published by Red Fox 2000

Printed and bound in Great Britain by Mackays of Chatham plc, Chatham, Kent

Papers used by Random House are natural, recyclable products made from wood
grown in sustainable forests. The manufacturing processes conform to the
environmental regulations of the country of origin.

The Random House Group Limited Reg. No. 954009
www.randomhouse.co.uk

ISBN 0 09 940 7620

QUENTIN BLAKE

The Laureate's Party

FIFTY FAVOURITE BOOKS CHOSEN BY THE FIRST CHILDREN'S LAUREATE

RED FOX

To my godchildren of three generations

Sue Evans

Kate Matthews

Charlie Murphy

An Invitation

In May 1999 I was appointed the first Children's Laureate. For the person who is chosen this means two things. To begin with there is a prize, a medal and money, in appreciation of everything by way of children's books, whether writing or drawing, that you have done so far. In addition to that you stay Children's Laureate for two years, and in that time you are invited to do whatever you feel is appropriate – by way of writing or talking or making visits, to encourage people to notice children's books and what is valuable about them. In fact you don't have to do anything; but some of the things you are invited to do are so interesting that it would be very hard to turn them down.

That is how it came about that, soon after the medal was hung round my neck, Random House, who are the publishers of my books and most of Roald Dahl's and many by Russell Hoban and Joan Aiken, asked me if I would like to put together a list of my fifty favourite books. I set to work. This is it.

You will understand immediately that this is not intended to be my choice of the fifty best children's books. There are people who could make such a list but I am not one of them – I just haven't read and seen enough. These are simply my favourites I think they are all good books, but I have chosen them for a number of different reasons. Some I read years ago, and remember with pleasure, and I have put them in even though I don't know if young readers today will react to them in the same way that I did then; others are books that I have only just recently discovered and I am still full of fresh enthusiasm for them. Some have an added interest because they are written or illustrated by my friends; some because I illustrated them myself and I thought they were particularly wonderful stories. In fact early on I asked if I could call this book *The Laureate's Party* because it did seem in some ways like a party –

one to which you invite your best friends, as well as people you haven't seen for a long time and want to get in touch with again, or people you don't know very well and would like to know better. The idea is that we shall all enjoy ourselves. At the beginning fifty books seemed a good number; and indeed so it is – except that now I have made the list I realise how many people I have left out. Amazing picture book people – John Burningham, Raymond Briggs, David McKee, Tony Ross, Lucy Cousins, Jill Murphy and Babette Cole. Famous writers like Jan Mark, William Mayne, J. K. Rowling and Jacqueline Wilson. So, for all those books which ought to be my favourites, and are yours, we have left you some pages to make your own list at the back of the book.

Quentin Blake

Picture
Books

The Tale of Two Bad Mice
Beatrix Potter

Beatrix Potter is one of those famous children's writers that I didn't really find out about until I was grown up – in fact I can see from the date in the front of my copy of this book that I bought it when I was thirty-four. What I so like about it is the way in which the mice are real characters and yet at the same time – because Beatrix Potter was a skilled natural history illustrator – very accurate and lifelike. If I needed another reason it might be that Beatrix Potter spent most of her early life in a house not five minutes from where I live. Alas, the house is gone now; but appropriately enough there is a school on the site, full of lots of lively and interesting children; and there is a picture of Peter Rabbit on the wall.

HUNCA MUNCA tried
every tin spoon in turn;
the fish was glued to the dish.

Then Tom Thumb lost his
temper. He put the ham in the
middle of the floor, and hit it
with the tongs and with the
shovel – bang, bang, smash, smash!

The ham flew all into pieces,
for underneath the shiny paint it
was made of nothing but plaster!

Little Tim and the Brave Sea Captain

Edward Ardizzone

I was lucky enough to meet Edward Ardizzone once or twice, many years ago; a white-haired patriarchal figure by then, spilling snuff down the front of his cardigan and full of wise remarks about drawing. I had not known his books when I was a child, but enjoyed them tremendously when I met them as a grown-up. There's a sort of simple but magical quality to all his work whether for children or adults and in the Little Tim books a wonderful sense of seaside light and seaside places.

The Captain would tell him about his voyages and sometimes give him a sip of his grog, which made Tim want to be a sailor more than ever.

Madeline
Ludwig Bemelmans

Somehow the *Madeline* books are not like any other children's books; you love Madeline and her friends "in two straight lines" without ever getting very close to them. Bemelmans wrote stories and drew pictures about unusual people, travel, hotels, cities. The backgrounds of *Madeline* are really paintings of Paris, and it is they that help to give this book and the others their special quality.

in they walked and then said, "Ahhh,"
when they saw the toys and candy
and the dollhouse from Papa.

What Can You Do With a Shoe?

Beatrice Schenk de Regniers
illustrated by Maurice Sendak

Maurice Sendak's most famous book is *Where the Wild Things Are*, which helped to change a lot of people's ideas about children's books, once they got used to it. But even before that - in fact right from the start - Maurice Sendak's illustrations were fascinating, and it is good to see a recent reissue of this book, which is alert to narrative possibilities and just full of life.

What can you do
What can you do
What can you do
| |
with a broom?

You can use it for a hair brush

Or a tooth brush

Or a bear brush
(If you've got a bear)

You can use it for a shoe brush

Or a glue brush

Or a chair brush
(I'm sure you've got a chair)

Now a broom would feel tickly
to a prickly porcupion

And it would seem quite scratchy
on the batchy of a lion.

Doctor De Soto
William Steig

I can remember, many years ago, first seeing William Steig's drawings in *The New Yorker* magazine; he liked doing cartoons about Small Fry as he put it – kids from the poorer parts of the city, Brooklyn and the Bronx. When he got to the age of about sixty he started to write and illustrate books for children. They have a special flavour and unexpectedness so that they don't seem quite like other people's stories, and I don't think that anyone else would write a story about a fox and some mice (Dr de Soto is a dentist) quite like this.

Recently, my interest in William Steig has been made even stronger because I was asked to illustrate a story by him. It is about a witch, and called Wizzil. I thought perhaps it was because he felt like a rest, but no; it was just that at the age of 90 he had too many other projects to get round to it. Wonderful man.

"This tooth will have to come out," Doctor De Soto announced. "But we can make you a new one."

"Just stop the pain," whimpered the fox, wiping some tears away.

Despite his misery, he realized he had a tasty little morsel in his mouth, and his jaw began to quiver. "Keep open!" yelled Doctor De Soto. "Wide open!" yelled his wife.

21

More!
Emma Chichester Clark

Emma Chichester Clark always seems to be able to make her pictures full of life and activity – look at all the leaping and jumping that goes on in *Follow My Leader* for instance – as well as a richness

"More!" shouted Billy to the booming of the drums.

of colour that you can often only find in less animated stories. I also like *More!* for an additional reason – it is very difficult to put a message or a lesson into a picture book, though many try to do it. Here it is done smilingly, without finger-wagging, as though it were the simplest thing in the world, and we all feel better for it.

There was crackling and crashing, banging and bashing.

The Story Of Little Babaji
Helen Bannerman
illustrated by Fred Marcellino

This is a new version of a book that has existed for a long time. The words were written by Helen Bannerman and they remain the same except for changes to names to make it clear that everybody in the story is Indian. The pictures are new. It's hard to muck about like this with a book that a lot of older people know already unless you are very clever, but Fred Marcellino is one of the best illustrators in the USA and he is brilliant. He captures the spirit of Little Babaji and he knows all about those self-important tigers.

And Little Babaji said, "Oh! Please Mr. Tiger, don't eat me up, and I'll give you my beautiful little Red Coat." So the Tiger said, "Very well, I won't eat you this time, but you must give me your beautiful little Red Coat."

Queenie the Bantam
Bob Graham

Actually I wanted to put *Crusher is Coming* as my favourite, but I can't find my copy (have I lent it to someone?) and at this moment I am told it is not available. Look out for it anyway. In the meantime I like *Queenie the Bantam* almost as much. Bob Graham draws as though nothing is happening, but everything is beautifully planned and observed, which means that this ordinary family is no more ordinary than – well – any other ordinary family.

It was Caitlin who found the egg that morning.
And the next morning. And the next.

Every morning Queenie made her journey from the
farm to Caitlin's house and back,

leaving the gift of a small brown egg.

Only once did they spy on Queenie laying
her egg, and never again.

"It didn't seem right," said Mum. "It seemed..."
"Private," said Dad.

The Necessary Cat

Nicola Bayley

This is not just a book for cat-lovers (though it is that too), it's more a collection of small books, of poems and sayings and other ingenuities, that have cats in them. Nicola Bayley is so skilful that she illustrates each of them in a different way; so this extract doesn't really tell you what the whole book is like. It needs to be pored over (or, if you like, pawed over) at leisure.

Cats Can Be...

Alien

Bashful

Cunning

Dim

Enormous

Foolish

Glorious

Hairy

Idle

Jolly

Kindly

The Sea-Thing Child
Russell Hoban
illustrated by Patrick Benson

When I first read *The Sea-Thing Child* it was a version
that had very few pictures – in fact no more than a
few decorations. That was at the time, years ago, when
I had just illustrated what is still one of my favourite
books, *How Tom Beat Captain Najork and his Hired
Sportsmen*. Russell Hoban always seems able to mean so
much and to suggest so much with very few words;
and now we can have *The Sea-Thing Child*
illustrated by Patrick Benson, who is extremely good
at drawing and captures not only the character of that
strange creature but also the atmosphere and feel of
sea and sky.

One day an albatross landed on the beach,
pulled out a little stubby pipe and sat down to
have a smoke. The fiddler crab hid among the
rocks but the sea-thing child came over to talk
to the albatross.

"Ahoy," said the albatross. "Nice beach you've
got here. Good landing-strip. Good fishing.
Good rocks. Nice place." He puffed big clouds
of smoke from his little black pipe and stared
out to sea with fearless eyes. "You don't happen
to play the fiddle or anything like that, do you?
I like a bit of music and fun when I'm ashore."

Clever Bill
William Nicholson

William Nicholson was a distinguished painter and poster-designer. In the 1920s he illustrated *The Velveteen Rabbit* by Margery Williams and soon after that he wrote and illustrated *Clever Bill*. They are both about toys which in different ways come to life; the second book has a wonderful degree of informality and energy, as well as a delightful lack of explanation. As – I'm ashamed to say – I didn't know it when I produced *Clown*, I came upon it with a special small thrill of pleasure.

and of course I cant leave clever
Bill Davis, and my purse — so

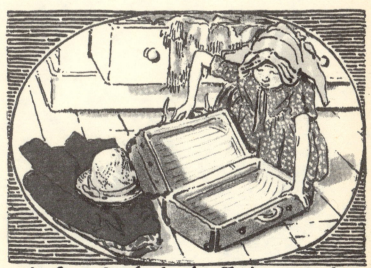

she brought the box her Father gave her

Le Carnet D'Albert
Bruno Heitz

It may seem rather perverse to include this book, but a lot of children do learn French, and if you want to know what it's like to be at school in France Albert's notebook, going from A to Z, tells you all about that, about parents and teachers, and a lot about the way our neighbours live today. Bruno Heitz (who is French, despite the German-sounding name) is one of the funniest and most imaginative of young children's book artists on the other side of the Channel.

Attention! L'instit n'est plus ce type à blouse grise, avec un sifflet autour du cou, et un crayon rouge dans la poche pour mettre des zéros.
Si vous en trouvez un comme ça, ne lui faites pas de mal:
c'est une espèce en voie de disparition!

L'instit d'aujourd'hui, lui...

★Les Instits are the Instituteurs or junior-school teachers.

Snow–white
Josephine Poole
illustrated by Angela Barrett

The great everlasting fairytales get re-told in such a variety of ways, not all very respectful (on occasion I have gone along with this in my illustrations). So it is good to encounter a book which takes one perfectly seriously. When you look at this version you feel that it is the real original Snow White. It has the confidence, both in words and pictures, to behave as though no other version has ever existed.

The queen could not find her way through the forest; besides, the wild beasts would certainly have eaten her. So, instead, she had to walk a long and weary way, over seven mountains, until at last she came to the cottage. She limped up the path crying, 'Collars and laces, belts and buttons! Pretty trifles for wives and maidens!'

Snow-white called from the window, 'Good-day, Granny. What have you to sell?'

Then the old woman held up the silken laces which so pleased Snow-white that she said to herself, What harm can there be in this good old woman? So she unbarred the door, and the pedlar woman glided in.

'What a beautiful figure you have, my dear, to be sure!' she exclaimed. This was true, though she only pretended to admire it. 'You shall have the laces as a present, only let me thread them for you.'

And with quick fingers she threaded the coloured silks into Snow-white's bodice, in and out, all the way up. Then she pulled them so tight that the poor girl could not breathe and fell senseless to the ground. 'So much for the fairest!' screeched the wicked queen, and she scuttled away in her old woman's shawl, like a spider.

Rose Blanche
Roberto Innocenti
text by Ian McEwan

Roberto Innocenti is an Italian who makes illustration of an extraordinary detail and realism. In his hands *Pinocchio* takes on a quite different air, in scenes of Tuscany in winter, from that of the original illustrations. His version of Charles Dickens's *A Christmas Carol* is also a remarkable tour de force, but for me the most surprising thing he has done is *Rose Blanche* which has to do with a town under the Nazi rule and a girl's discovery of Jewish children in a concentration camp. What is striking about this is that it combines sensitivity and discretion of portrayal with telling realistic details; fiction with some of the expressive powers of documentary.

Rose Blanche took a short-cut through the forest where bare branches scratched her face. The road was below her the lorry was a long way ahead. She was so tired, she felt like giving up.

Then she stumbled into a clearing and could hardly believe what she saw.

The Last Giants
François Place

This is a picture book for all ages, except (for once) the very small. François Place is an extraordinarily skilled French illustrator and (like Jules Verne) he has recounted the story of a nineteenth century British explorer. The giants he discovers are a wonderful invention, full of meaning. The conclusion of the story is (unfortunately for us) all too relevant to today. In many ways it resembles *The Lost World*, which you will find later in this book, but it's both sadder and more poetical.

There were nine of them: five Giants and four Giantesses. They were covered from head to foot – including their tongues and teeth – with a dizzying maze of extremely complex lines, curves, twinings, spirals, and speckles. Given time, one could discern recognizable images within this fantastic labyrinth: trees, plants, animals, flowers, rivers, oceans - a veritable symphony of the Earth that echoed the music of their

40

nightly invocations. To think that I had but two notebooks left in which to record all this! I was forced to write and draw so minutely that my pages began to look like the skins of the Giants themselves.

For their part, the Giants found watching me work hugely amusing. It was a spectacle they never tired of, which led me to realize that none of them knew how to draw.

A Ruined House
Mick Manning

What I like so much about this book is that it doesn't treat subjects like history and insects and birdwatching separately, but puts them all together as they are in life, so that when you look at this ruined house you learn something about how people once lived there as well as about how owls and beetles live there now. And because these are drawings with a personal quality, that might have been made on the spot, they also seem to convey something of Mick Manning's feelings about this interesting place.

It's dark indoors, but if you're very quiet you might see a family of barn owls peering down at you from a fireplace high on the wall.

The high-up fireplace is a clue. Before the floor collapsed, there must have been an upstairs in the house.

Story Books

The Eighteenth Emergency
Betsy Byars

One of the tasks of an illustrator is to produce jackets for books which otherwise don't have illustrations. Sometimes you are only told a brief account of the story, and you have to do the best you can with that; but it's really much more satisfactory from every point of view if you are given the whole book. There is the added advantage that you can lie in bed all morning reading it with the comfortable knowledge that you are actually *working*.

I have met many new books like this, and one I remember well is *The Eighteenth Emergency*.

> Emergency Four – Crocodile Attack. When attacked by a crocodile, prop a stick in its mouth and the crocodile is helpless.
>
> At one time this had been his own favourite emergency. He had spent a lot of time dreaming of tricking crocodiles. He had imagined himself a tornado in the water, handing out the sticks like party favours. "Take that and that and that!" The stunned crocodiles, mouths propped open, had dragged themselves away. For the rest of their lives they had avoided children with sticks in their hands. "Hey, no!" his dream crocodiles had cried, "Let that kid alone. He's got sticks, man, *sticks!*"
>
> Abruptly he turned his head towards the sofa. The smile which had come to his face when he had remembered the crocodiles now faded. He pulled a thread in the slip cover. The material began to pucker,

and he stopped pulling and smoothed it out. Then he took a pencil from his pocket and wrote in tiny letters on the wall PULL THREAD IN CASE OF BOREDOM and drew a little arrow to the sofa.

The words blurred suddenly, and he let the pencil drop behind the sofa. He lay back down. Hammerman was in his mind again, and he closed his eyes. He tried hard to think of the days when he and Ezzie had been ready to handle crocodiles and bulls, quick-sand and lions. It seemed a long time ago.

The Winter Sleepwalker
Joan Aiken

I first met Joan Aiken when I was asked to do the pictures for a story which she had written specially for BBC Television about a little girl called Arabel and her raven, Mortimer. Later on there were more stories about Arabel and Mortimer, which were not only television programmes but also made into books, with new illustrations. I got to love Mortimer very much indeed because he was very enjoyable to draw and full of uncontrolled urges and unexpectedness, so that when he felt like it he would eat things; often quite large metal things, like the escalator on the underground. And then more recently I was lucky enough to be asked to illustrate *The Winter Sleepwalker*, something quite different – a collection of new fairy tales is what it is really I suppose, with magic and telephones and motorbikes and monsters.

from Blazing Shadows

One day, an old lady was walking slowly along the village street of High Blowfield. She walked very slowly, leaning on a broken stick. She was so bent that her head hung down, almost to her knees.

As she walked, she grumbled.

'Nasty cold day. Birds singing much too loud. Wind blowing far too hard. Too many cars. Too many people. Too many dogs. Too many children.'

Nothing was right for her.

The birds flew away in fright as she passed them. And every dog she met either snarled or growled, or ran off, whining, with its tail between its legs. One big black dog, sitting behind a garden gate, let out such a volley of barks that the old woman turned round, glared at it fiercely out of her red-rimmed eyes, and pointed her skinny finger at it.

The dog turned into a small prickly holly tree, growing (most awkwardly for its owner) right in the middle of the garden path.

'That'll teach *you*,' said the old lady.

One of two children giggled nervously, and stared at her. But they did it from the far side of the road, a safe distance away.

'I'd set my geese on you, if I had them here!' the old lady hissed at the children, sounding rather like a goose herself, as she stretched out her skinny neck, and shook her broken stick.

'That's the witch from Shadow Wood,' a boy whispered to his cousin, who was a stranger to the village. 'She could turn you into a poisonous toadstool, as soon as look at you. Better keep out of her way.'

Underrunners
Margaret Mahy

Margaret Mahy lives in New Zealand, but she belongs to the world. I first got to know about her work when I illustrated two stories which appeared together as one book: *The Great Piratical Rumbustification* and *The Librarian and The Robbers.* These are wild and funny stories; I don't really know what age of reader they are best suited for, but I know that all librarians ought to read the second one because Margaret Mahy was once a librarian and this story tells you the most important things about running a library, especially one for children. I found the same appetite for humour and language in *Non-Stop Nonsense*; not nonsense at all, a lot of the time, just wisdom skewed round sideways a bit.

But there is another whole side to Margaret Mahy's writing – novels for older children. *Underrunners* is one of them – funny and exciting, but at the same time looking at human relationships and dilemmas, such as everyone encounters, though not perhaps in such a striking and gripping way.

> Winola laughed. Her teeth were white and sharp - fox's teeth, thought Tris, though he'd never seen a fox in his life.
>
> 'There's someone after me. I have to have an escape route planned.'
>
> 'Who's after you?' Tris asked. But Winola's eyes suddenly lost their sharpness. Her whole face went vague. Her eyelids came down and half covered her

astonishing light-grey eyes, almost as if she were suddenly on the point of going to sleep.

'Someone!' she said, even sounding drowsy. 'An evil villain, okay?'

'We should get someone on to him,' Tris remarked. 'Selsey Firebone,' he suggested daringly, surprising himself.

Her face grew sharp and foxy again.

'We need someone tough,' she said. 'Someone with a Lee Enfield 303 or a nuclear cannon. What about Selsey Firebone?'

'Selsey's really tough!' cried Tris quickly. 'He's got scars criss-crossed all over him.' As he spoke he found himself imagining something new about Selsey. 'He's had a lot of skin grafts so he's got black skin and brown skin and pink skin...'

'How come he's criss-crossed in scars if he's so tough?' Winola asked. 'I mean, how come anyone gets near enough to scar him?'

'Well, some of his enemies are tough too - tough and clever,' Tris began, suddenly eager to describe some Selsey adventure. Winola interrupted him.

'Fiendishly clever!' she exclaimed reprovingly, as if he had got some part of the story wrong. 'Say they're *fiendishly* clever!' Then she laughed. Tris paused and laughed too. By laughing they were somehow agreeing that this was a game, without actually having to say so.

Uncle and the Treacle Trouble
J. P. Martin

Uncle is an enormously rich elephant who normally wears a purple dressing gown. He has many employees and hangers-on and lives in a huge castle of many towers. When I was first asked to draw Uncle, many years ago, I wasn't quite sure how much I liked him; there was no escaping the fact that he *was* rather pompous. However, I revelled in the extraordinary number of characters, especially the Badfort crowd - a dirty, bristly, badly-behaved collection of layabouts with names like Beaver Hateman, Hitmouse and Jellytussle; and I soon realised that J. P. Martin (who was a Methodist minister and had told all these stories to his grandchildren) relished the contrast and conflict that resulted as much as I did.

Time has passed since these books first appeared. In recent years I have regularly received letters (so have the publishers) from people who read these stories as children but are now grown up and have children of their own. They wanted the books for *them*, and couldn't find them. Now they are about to be reissued and the gallery of eccentrics and their exploits once more put on show. Watch out for that Hitmouse, though – he's a nasty little piece of work.

> Uncle owns so much property, and has so many people working for him, that every post brings cheques for rent or for crops of maize and bananas, or else complaints from tenants, most of whom he has never seen.

He always hates being disturbed when he is dealing with the post, so he frowned heavily when the light from the window was blocked by a large rough figure which had climbed up on the window-sill.

It was Beaver Hateman, who in the clear light of early morning was a shocking sight. He was wearing a tattered sack suit, and an old top hat above hair which looked like a bundle of badly stacked straw. He carried a stone club under one arm.

"Hi, Unc!" he shouted.

Uncle took off his glasses.

"Will you kindly address me properly," he said.

"Oh, shut up!" said Hateman. "You're not getting a lot of bowing and scraping from me! I've come to complain about that great fat friend of yours who was trespassing on my land last night!"

"I have no fat friend," said Uncle, with dignity.

Featherbrains
John Yeoman

The first children's book I ever illustrated was by John Yeoman, who wrote it specially for me. It was a collection of stories called *A Drink of Water* and it has not been available for many years. This has not prevented us from going back and using bits of it again from time to time. One of the stories I have just reillustrated as a picture book called *The Heron and the Crane*. And though most of John Yeoman's stories are intended as picture books he has written some longer stories such as *Featherbrains*, which is about two chickens who escape by accident from a battery farm, and their adventures in the outside world. Needless to say their exploits are very funny to draw, because John Yeoman has an eye for visual possibilities. As with so many animal stories, this one is not simply about animals and, as one of the friends of the author who knows about such things suggested, a copy could usefully be given to anyone about to leave prison.

Bessie was already scratching around. Just as the jack-daw had said, she found it quite easy – and, for some reason, very exciting.

"Look at Bessie," Flossie cried; "she's dancing!"

In no time Bessie had unearthed a little tangle of worms. Summoning up their courage, the two hens each picked up one of the smallest and gulped it down.

There was a pause while they thought about it.

"You know," said Bessie finally, "they taste much nicer than food."

"You're right, Bessie," said Flossie. "But they can't be good for us, can they? I mean, they've been on the dirty ground and they don't have any special extras."

"Extras?" asked the jackdaw.

"Oh, yes," said Bessie; "our chicken-feed always has extras to make us fit and strong..."

"...like bits of chopped-up beak..." said Flossie.

"...and minced feathers..."

"...and medicines," said Flossie.

"Why medicines?" asked the jackdaw.

"So that we don't feel unwell," Bessie explained.

"You mean, no one ever feels unwell in that shed?" asked the jackdaw.

"Oh, yes; people are ill all the time," said Flossie.

Emil and the Detectives
Erich Kästner
illustrated by Walter Trier

This book is one of my favourites and not just for the story but also for the way the words are perfectly matched by the drawings of Walter Trier. They appear to be very simple but they are satisfying to look at and full of meaning and atmosphere. Trier was a very gifted artist whose work is little known in England nowadays. Happily his collaboration with Erich Kästner is celebrated every year in the Maschler award, established by Kurt Maschler, their original publisher, and which is given to the book in which the words and pictures go best together.

These miserable reflections were interrupted by a motor-horn which honked loudly just behind him. It made him jump, but when he looked round there was only a boy standing there, laughing.

"All right, don't get the wind up," he said.

"It sounded as though there was a motor right behind me," Emil said.

"Silly chump, that was me. You can't belong round here or you'd know that. I always carry a motor-horn in my trouser pocket. Everyone knows me and my motor-horn."

"I live in Neustadt," Emil explained. "I've only just come from the station."

"Oh, up from the country!" said the boy. "I suppose

that's why you're wearing those awful clothes."

"You take that back," said Emil furiously, "or I'll knock you down."

"Keep your hair on," said the boy with the motor-horn good-naturedly. "It's too hot to fight... though if you really want to, I'm willing."

"I don't specially," Emil said. "Let's put it off. I've no time now," and he glanced quickly up at the café to make sure that Mr Grundeis was still there.

"I should have thought you had plenty of time," the boy retorted, "hanging about here with your outside suitcase and that great cauliflower! You looked as though you were playing hide and seek with yourself. I can't say you seem to me in much of a hurry."

"As a matter of fact," said Emil, "I'm keeping my eye on a thief."

"What!" exclaimed the boy with the motor-horn. "A thief? What has he stolen? Who from?"

"Me," said Emil, feeling quite important again.

Five Children and It
E. Nesbit

I suppose that everybody knows that E. Nesbit was a woman writer. For part of her life she lived on Romney Marsh in Kent, which is one of my favourite places; but much more important than that is the fact that she was one of the first people who showed children in books having lively, intelligent conversations among themselves, and getting on on their own. Her stories start in everyday life (though it is the everyday life of a hundred years ago, so in some ways strange to us) and, via magic and her imagination, take off into extraordinary happenings. The magic in *Five Children and It* is provided by the Psammead or Sand Fairy who is immensely old and hairy and strange-looking and in that and other respects a sort of *difficult grown-up*.

> Then Anthea cried out, '*I'm* not afraid. Let me dig,' and fell on her knees and began to scratch like a dog does when he suddenly remembered where it was that he buried his bone.
>
> 'Oh, I felt fur,' she cried, half laughing and half crying. 'I did indeed! I did!' when suddenly a dry husky voice in the sand made them all jump back, and their hearts jumped nearly as fast as they did.
>
> 'Let me alone,' it said. And now everyone heard the voice and looked at the others to see if they had too.
>
> 'But we want to see you,' said Robert bravely.
>
> 'I wish you'd come out,' said Anthea, also taking courage.

'Oh, well – if that's your wish,' the voice said, and
the sand stirred and spun and scattered, and something
brown and furry and fat came rolling out into the
hole and the sand fell off it, and it sat there yawning
and rubbing the ends of its eyes with its hands.

'I believe I must have dropped asleep,' it said,
stretching itself.

The children stood round the hole in a ring, looking
at the creature they had found. It was worth looking
at. Its eyes were on long horns like a snail's eyes, and it
could move them in and out like telescopes; it had
ears like a bat's ears, and its tubby body was shaped
like a spider's and covered with thick soft fur; its legs
and arms were furry too, and it had hands and feet
like a monkey's.

'What on earth is it?' Jane said. 'Shall we take it
home?'

The thing turned its long eyes to look at her, and
said: 'Does she always talk nonsense or is it only the
rubbish in her head that makes her silly?'

'She doesn't mean to be silly,' Anthea said gently;
'we none of us do, whatever you may think! Don't be
frightened; we don't want to hurt you, you know.'

'Hurt *me!*' it said. '*Me* frightened? Upon my word!
Why, you talk as if I were nobody in particular.' All
its fur stood out like a cat's when it is going to fight.

The Indian in the Cupboard
Lynne Reid Banks

This is the story of the boy Omri and how he discovers that a toy Red Indian that he owns can sometimes come to life. Although this has the appearance of a fairly simple idea there are all kinds of interesting and unexpected things to be discovered in it, not just the change of scale between the two main characters. It also brings up questions about being responsible for people and how we expect people to behave. And the Red Indian, Little Bull, is, if you like, another *difficult grown up*. I find it fascinating.

In the morning there was no doubt about it. The noise actually woke him.

He lay perfectly still in the dawn light staring at the cupboard, from which was now coming a most extraordinary series of sounds. A pattering; a tapping; a scrabbling; and – surely? – a high-pitched noise like – well, almost like a tiny voice.

To be truthful, Omri was petrified. Who wouldn't be? Undoubtedly there was something alive in that cupboard. At last, he put out his hand and touched it. He pulled very carefully, the door was tight shut. But as he pulled the cupboard moved, just slightly. The noise from inside instantly stopped.

He lay still for a long time, wondering. Had he imagined it? The noise did not start again. At last he cautiously turned the key and opened the cupboard door.

The Indian was gone.

Omri sat up sharply and peered into the dark corners. Suddenly he saw him. But he wasn't on the shelf any more, he was in the bottom of the cupboard. And he wasn't standing upright. He was crouching in the darkest corner, half hidden by the front of the cupboard. And he was alive.

Omri knew that immediately. To begin with, though the Indian was trying to keep perfectly still – as still as Omri had kept, lying in bed a moment ago – he was breathing heavily. His bare, bronze shoulders rose and fell, and were shiny with sweat. The single feather sticking out of the back of his headband quivered, as if the Indian were trembling. And as Omri peered closer, and his breath fell on the tiny huddled figure, he saw it jump to its feet; its minute hand made a sudden, darting movement towards its belt and came to rest clutching the handle of a knife smaller than the shaft of a drawing-pin.

Neither Omri nor the Indian moved for perhaps a minute and a half. They hardly breathed either. They just stared at each other. The Indian's eyes were black and fierce and frightened. His lower lip was drawn down from shining white teeth, so small you could scarcely see them except when they caught the light. He stood pressed against the inside wall of the cupboard, clutching his knife, rigid with terror, but defiant.

The Granny Project
Anne Fine

And here is a third book about a *difficult grown-up*, and you might expect that it would be rather heavy going because there is no magic or fantasy or adventure in it. However, it is simply the story of the Harris family and what they are to do, and think, and feel, about their very aged grandmother. But this is written by Anne Fine, so that though it addresses the serious reality of the situation it is also funny and moving and full of unexpectedness. With what dash she attacks it all – there is no hanging about. Everything is done in short scenes as if it were a film – and notice just how much of it is done in lively and convincing dialogue. Raising to the spirits!

"Well?" Ivan said. "Sophie?"

"Listen," said Sophie. " This Project that was set last week – "

"For Social Science?"

"Yes."

"Well?"

"You and me, Ivan, we'll team up for it. We'll work together, doing a joint Project, double the length."

"On?"

"Ageing people in the community."

Ivan began to grin. Tanya and Nicholas looked

blank. Sophie went on:

"We'll get the statistics stuff from newspapers and reference books. That won't take long. But half the Project, a good half of it, will be a fairly vivid and uncensored description – "

Ivan broke in:

"Of one particular family!"

"An illustration of the fundamental stresses – "

"Features –"

"*And* issues,"

"The economic,"

"Social,"

"And psycho-social –"

"Pressures which underlie this growing trend – "

"Of taking ageing – "

"Non-functional! – "

"Members of the family unit,"

"And relocating them,"

"Along with their peers,"

"In Leisure Homes!"

"A case study,"

"In *depth*,"

"Of one particular set – "

"Of family dynamics."

"The *Harris* Family!"

"That's it."

"Oh, well done, Sophie! Well, done! Well done!"

Ivan's eyes shone, Sophie looked rather proud of herself. Tanya and Nicholas, uncomprehending and forlorn, began to complain.

"What about *us*?"

Stuart Little
E. B. White
illustrated by Garth Williams

E. B. White spent most of his life writing for the famous American magazine, *The New Yorker.* He wrote only three children's books and one of them, *Charlotte's Web*, is very good indeed and I suppose pretty well everybody knows about it and likes it. But it is sometimes interesting to find out about the *other* books of the writer of a book you like. It is an unusual book about a couple who have a *mouse* for a child, and about how he grows up and how he lived and how he falls in love with a bird. I like it very much although I am not quite perfectly sure what it all means. Like *Charlotte's Web* it has very good drawings by Garth Williams.

When Mrs. Frederick C. Little's second son arrived, everybody noticed that he was not much bigger than a mouse. The truth of the matter was, the baby looked very much like a mouse in every way. He was only about two inches high; and he had a mouse's sharp nose, a mouse's tail, a mouse's whiskers, and the pleasant, shy manner of a mouse. Before he was many days old he was not only looking like a mouse but acting like one, too – wearing a grey hat and carrying a small cane. Mr. and Mrs. Little named him Stuart, and Mr. Little made him a tiny bed out of four clothespins and a cigarette box.

Unlike most babies, Stuart could walk as soon as he was born. When he was a week old he could climb lamps by shinnying up the cord. Mrs. Little saw right away that the infant clothes she had provided were unsuitable, and she set to work and made him a fine little blue worsted suit with patch pockets in which he could keep his handkerchief, his money, and his keys. Every morning, before Stuart dressed, Mrs. Little went into his room and weighed him on a small scale which was really meant for weighing letters. At birth Stuart could have been sent by first class mail for three cents, but his parents preferred to keep him rather than send him away; and when, at the age of a month, he had gained only a third of an ounce, his mother was so worried she sent for the doctor.

The doctor was delighted with Stuart and said that it was very unusual for an American family to have a mouse. He took Stuart's temperature and found that it was 98.6, which is normal for a mouse. He also examined Stuart's chest and heart and looked into his ear solemnly with a flashlight. (Not every doctor can look into a mouse's ear without laughing.) Everything seemed to be all right, and Mrs. Little was pleased

The Box of Delights
John Masefield

John Masefield was at one time a very well-known poet, and from 1930 to 1967 he was the Poet Laureate, though, with the exception of a few poems like *Cargoes*, not many people read his poetry now. Perhaps because despite its merits the poetry seems rather old-fashioned. Strangely, two of the children's books he wrote are in many ways more imaginative and filled with unusual and dream-like effects than his poetry. They are *The Box of Delights* and *The Midnight Folk* and are both about the adventures of the boy Kay Harker and the plotting of a strange figure of evil called Abner Brown. What is fascinating about them is the way that they mix the old and the modern, dream and reality in such an extraordinary way that quite often you can't tell which is which. My guess is that Joan Aiken, Philip Pullman, J. K. Rowling and many other writers would not be quite the same without *The Box of Delights*.

He had never before realised how troublesome a sheet of paper can be when it is rather bigger than a blanket, naturally of a stiff quality, and already crumpled from some days in a pocket. As he drew it out, opened it and bent back the crumpled corners, he became suddenly aware that the Wolves were Running with a little whirring snarl. Little motor-cars with wolf heads rushed at him from different points of the cave, and snapped at him.

"Don't heed those, Master Kay," Cole Hawlings said.

It was not so easy not to heed them, for they came at him with such malice that the snapping of their bonnets was very terrifying. Any bonnet of them all was big and strong enough to snap him down into the engines, where he would have been champed up in no time.

For about half a minute he wrestled with the paper, trying to get it flat. The little motor-cars snapped at him all the time. Snap, snap. One of them would run behind him and snap at his ankles, while another darted at him to bite his toes. Then he realised that though they snapped very near, they never really bit him; he himself was in some way safe, they could only annoy and hinder. Presently, he straightened out one corner of the paper; instantly, one of these snapping motor-cars rushed over it, crushed it back.

"Hit them with the pencil, Master Kay," Cole Hawlings said. This was very much like saying, "Hit them with the lamp-post," or "Whack them with the telegraph pole."

"I don't think I can lift the pencil," Kay said; "it's too heavy."

"Well try now," Cole said.

Kay tried, and to his great delight found that he could lift this great fir-tree of a pencil. For a moment he felt like one of those heroes at the Scottish Games tossing the fir-tree for a haggis. As the motor-car came at him once more, trying to force the paper from under him, he smote the bonnet a lusty blow. The car at once upset and rolled over and over and over with a puncture in all four wheels. A little whimper of pain came from its klaxon, and the other little wolf motor-cars drew to one side and clashed their bonnets at Kay, snap, snap.

Northern Lights
Philip Pullman

Northern Lights is the first of a trilogy;three books under the general title *His Dark Materials*. They are all part of the same story which takes place both in our world and another which in many ways is like ours but strangely parallel in a complicated way. Even this first book on its own is extraordinarily rich in thoughts, characters, ideas and adventures.

When Lyra woke up, the moon was high in the sky, and everything in sight was silver-plated, from the rolling surface of the clouds below to the frost-spears and icicles on the rigging of the balloon.

Roger was sleeping, and so were Lee Scoresby and the bear. Beside the basket, however, the witch-queen was flying steadily.

"How far are we from Svalbard?" Lyra said.

"If we meet no winds, we shall be over Svalbard in twelve hours or so."

"Where are we going to land?"

"It depends on the weather. We'll try to avoid the cliffs, though. There are creatures living there who prey on anything that moves. If we can, we'll set you down in the interior, away from Iofur Raknison's palace."

"What's going to happen when I find Lord Asriel? Will he want to come back to Oxford, or what? I don't know if I ought to tell him I know he's my father, neither. He might want to pretend he's still my uncle. I don't hardly know him at all."

"He won't want to go back to Oxford, Lyra. It seems that there is something to be done in another world, and Lord Asriel is the only one who can bridge the gulf between that world and this. But he needs something to help him."

"The alethiometer!" Lyra said. "The Master of Jordan gave it to me and I thought there was something he wanted to say about Lord Asriel, except he never had the chance. I knew he didn't *really* want to poison him. Is he going to read it and see how to make the bridge? I bet I could help him. I can probably read it as good as anyone now."

"I don't know," said Serafina Pekkala. "How he'll do it, and what his task will be, we can't tell. There are powers who speak to us, and there are powers above them; and there are secrets even from the most high."

"The alethiometer would tell me! I could read it now..."

But it was too cold; she would never have managed to hold it. She bundled herself up and pulled the hood tight against the chill of the wind, leaving only a slit to look through. Far ahead, and a little below, the long rope extended from the suspension-ring of the balloon, pulled by six or seven witches sitting on their cloud-pine branches. The stars shone as bright and cold and hard as diamonds.

Rumplestiltskin
Carol Ann Duffy
illustrated by Markéta Prachatická

Folktales and fairytales never stop being fascinating, and this collection of retellings is a particularly good one, for two reasons. One is that they keep to the spirit of the originals – they're really tough and frightening, and you can tell that they come from long ago. At the same time they have an urgent use of present day speech, chosen with an eye to sound and impact, so that it isn't hard to imagine these stories being told – perhaps round the fire in winter – rather than being written down.

> The Queen sat up all night, searching her brains for his name like someone sieving for gold. She went through every single name she could think of. She sent out a messenger to ask everywhere in the land for all the names that could be spoken, sung or spelled. On the next day, when the little man came, she recited the whole alphabet of names that she'd learned, starting with Balthasar, Casper, Melchior... But to each one the little man piped, "That's not my name."
> On the second day, she sent servants all round the neighbourhood to ferret out more names and she tried all the weird and wacky ones on the little man. "Perhaps you're called Shortribs or Sheepshanks or Lacelegs."
> But he always said, "That's not my name."
> On the third day, the messenger came back and said,

"I haven't managed to find a single new name, but as I came near to a high mountain at the end of forest, the place where fox and hare wish each other goodnight, I spied a small hut. There was a fire burning outside it and round the flames danced a bizarre little man. He hopped on one leg and bawled,

"Bake today! Tomorrow brew!
Then I'll take the young Queen's child!
She will cry and wish she knew
That RUMPELSTILTSKIN's how I'm styled."

Esio Trot
Roald Dahl

I couldn't do this book without including a work by
Roald Dahl, but the problem is to decide which one.
Drawing those two horrible dirty people in *The Twits*,
for instance, was so enjoyable. So was, at the other end
of the scale of likeability, drawing Sophie and the BFG.
In the end I have chosen *Esio Trot* for two reasons.
One, that it was fascinating to arrange the illustrations
– looking *up* to Mr Hoppy's flat, looking *down* from it
– and fun to do the tortoise's reactions. But more
importantly, too, is that, unusually for Roald Dahl,
there are no baddies – and there is the unmentioned
joke that all Mr Hoppy's practical masculine ingenuity
is used to get over a problem that doesn't exist. "Oh,"
says Mrs Silver when he finally proposes, "I thought
you would never ask." I think you would have to be
rather happy to write this story.

Mrs Silver did just that, and in half a minute she was back holding the tortoise in both hands and waving it above her head and shouting, "Guess what, Mr Hoppy! Guess what! He weighs twenty-seven ounces! He's twice as big as he was before! Oh you darling!" she cried, stroking the tortoise. "Oh, you great big wonderful boy! Just look what clever Mr Hoppy has done for you!"

Great Northern?
Arthur Ransome

One thing I liked about Arthur Ransome's books when I read them as a boy was that there was plenty of room to move about in them; not only the hills of the Lake District and Scotland and the expanses of the Norfolk Broads, but also in the extent of the writing, so that the books were long enough for you to feel that you were living in them. The effect is increased by Ransome's own drawings which, though they are in a way amateurish, give you a very good sense of the scale in relation to the characters, of boats and lakes and hills. *Great Northern?* is a special favourite because it is about the pleasures of birdwatching, as well as the urgency of frustrating the destructive attempts of a pseudo-scientific egg-collector. Thank goodness for the RSPB.

> The swimming bird, with one dive after another,
> had come nearly half way from the island towards
> the place where Dick lay hid. He was getting a better
> view of it each time it came to the top of the water.
> Its head seemed very dark on the top, and the whole
> bird seemed even larger than he had thought it at first
> sight. It dived, and came up a minute later with a fish,
> struggled with it on the surface, swallowed it, sipped
> water, and swam nearer still. Dick was puzzled, but he
> knew very well that nothing is more difficult to judge
> than the size of things seen at a distance through a
> telescope. The bird dived again. Dick watched the spot

where it had gone under, but it must have been swim-
ming straight towards him. When it came up it was
no more than thirty yards off, and Dick was so startled
that he nearly shouted aloud.

"It's a Great Northern," he said to himself, and had
added it to his list before he remembered that Great
Northern Divers did not nest in Great Britain.

"It can't be," he said to himself. "But it isn't a Black-
throated."

He made rather a mess of the pages in his notebook
where he had written of those birds. He had drawn a
line through "Black-throated" and had written "Great
Northern" before, remembering that there could be
no nest, he put a line through that. He jammed down
some question marks.

Again he had a good view of the bird and saw
clearly that had two patches of black and white stripes
on its dark neck.

"It *is* a Great Northern," he said, made another entry
in his book, and then, looking out once more at that
dark blob of the bird on the island, still where it was,
he crossed it out again and turned over a fresh page.

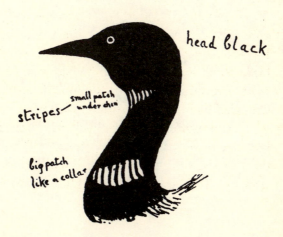

King of Shadows
Susan Cooper

King of Shadows is about a shift of time that takes an American boy, Nat Field, back to take part in a production of *A Midsummer Night's Dream* with Shakespeare at the Globe Theatre. Fascinating, especially if you know a bit about the play. I was one of those people lucky enough to take part in Shakespeare plays when I was at school, and once you get the idea of it, it never goes away. And, of course, as well as reading this book you can now go and see the reconstruction of the Globe itself on Bankside.

Will Shakespeare smiled at me, moving to stage centre, and instantly he became Oberon, shouting after Titania, who has had her row with him and left in a huff. It was the start of our first scene together in *A Midsummer Night's Dream*.

'Well, go thy way; thou shalt not from this grove
Til I torment thee for this injury.
My gentle Puck, come hither.'

He beckoned me. Instinctively I obeyed the direction that Arby would give me four hundred years from now, and I went to him in a double somersault. I came up on my feet close enough for him to touch me. Shakespeare, surprised, laughed aloud. He made no comment he just went on through the scene, until he reached Oberon's speech about the magic flower that he wants fetched ('love in idleness', which he told me later was another name for a pansy). He sent me off to find it.

*'Fetch me this herb and be thou here again
Ere the leviathan can swim a league.'*

I was hopping around him like a bird longing to fly.

*'I'll put a girdle round about the earth
In forty minutes.'*

That was my exit line. I remembered Arby's direction, and I paused, uncertainly. 'Can I go off through the house?'

'Through the house?' Shakespeare said.

I pointed.

'No, no,' he said firmly. 'That is for clowns, and not clowns of my liking. Thy place is the stage.'

'Tumbling, then?'

'Show me.'

I threw myself hand over hand and cartwheeled across the stage towards the exit door. Arby had worked this out too, for a different scene, and I knew it looked good from the front. Shakespeare chuckled.

'Very pretty,' he said.

The Lost World
Arthur Conan Doyle

The Lost World was written nearly a hundred years ago, and was one of the first books to explore the excitement and possibilities of adventure in encountering dinosaurs. Conan Doyle knew all about telling a story (he was also the creator of Sherlock Holmes) and I think the exploits of the extraordinary Professor Challenger and his companions are still gripping today. As a boy's story for men, or a man's story for boys of its time (as the author admits), women hardly get a look in at all – but perhaps part of the interest of reading the book is also to note the differences of behaviour and expectation between then and now. In that way too it is a description of a lost world.

That night (our third in Maple White Land) we had an experience which left a fearful impression upon our minds, and made us thankful that Lord John had worked so hard in making our retreat impregnable. We were all sleeping round our dying fire when we were aroused - or, rather, I should say, shot out of our slumbers - by a succession of the most frightful cries and screams to which I have ever listened. I know no sound to which I could compare this amazing tumult, which seemed to come from some spot within a few hundred yards of our camp. It was as ear-splitting as any whistle of a railway-engine; but whereas the whistle is a clear, mechanical, sharp-edged sound, this was far deeper in volume and vibrant with the uttermost strain of agony and horror. We clapped our hands to our ears to shut out that nerve-shaking appeal. A cold sweat broke out over my body, and my heart turned sick at the misery of it. All the woes of tortured life, all its stupendous indictments of high heaven, its innumerable sorrows, seemed to be centred and condensed into that one dreadful, agonized cry. And then, under this high-pitched, ringing sound there was another, more intermittent, a low, deep-chested laugh, a growling, throaty gurgle of merriment which formed a grotesque accompaniment to the shriek with which it was blended. For three or four minutes on end the fearsome duet continued, while all the foliage rustled with the rising of startled birds. Then it shut off as suddenly as it began. For a long time we sat in horrified silence. Then Lord John threw a bundle of twigs upon the fire, and their red glare lit up the intent faces of my companions and flickered over the great boughs above our head.

'What was it?' I whispered.

'We shall know in the morning,' said Lord John. 'It was close to us - not farther than the glade.'

'We have been privileged to overhear a prehistoric tragedy, the sort of drama which occurred among the reeds upon the border of some Jurassic lagoon, when the greater dragon pinned the lesser among the slime,' said Challenger, with more solemnity than I had ever heard in his voice. 'It was surely well for man that he came late in the order of creation.

Kensuke's Kingdom
Michael Morpurgo

Islands have played an important part in literature – think of Robert Louis Stevenson's *Treasure Island*, or Daniel Defoe's *Robinson Crusoe*, or William Golding's *Lord of the Flies* – clearly they also mean a lot to Michael Morpurgo, because he has written about them more than once. There must be something that both focuses and stimulates the imagination in a place that you can draw a line round. Certainly the experiences of Michael Morpurgo's young hero when he is shipwrecked on an island only inhabited by Kensuke, the old Japanese left there since the war years, are full of exciting incident as well as thoughts and observations about the ways people live together.

To see Kensuke at his work was always a wonder to me – he was so intent, so concentrated in everything he did. But watching him paint was best of all. To begin with he would only let me kneel beside him and watch. I could sense that in this, too, he liked his privacy, that he did not want to be disturbed. On the table in front of him he put out three saucers: one saucer of octopus ink (for Kensuke, octopuses were not just for eating), one saucer of water and another for mixing. He always held his brush very upright and very steady in his hand, fingers down one side, thumb on the other. He would kneel bent over his work, his beard almost touching the shell he was painting – I think perhaps he was a little short-sighted. I would watch him for hours on end, marvelling at the delicacy of his work, at the sureness of his touch.

Then one rainy afternoon – and when it rained, how it rained – I found he'd set out a shell for me, my own three saucers and my own paint-brush. He took such a delight in teaching me, in my every clumsy attempt. I remember early on I tried to paint the jellyfish that had attacked me. He laughed out loud at that, but not in a mocking way, rather in recognition, in memory, of what had brought us together. I had always liked to draw, but from Kensuke I learned to love it, that to draw or paint I first had to observe well, then set out the form of the picture in my head and send it down my arm through the tip of the brush and on to the shell. He taught me all this entirely without speaking. He simply showed me.

Poetry
Books

Mind Your Own Business
Michael Rosen

Mind Your Own Business was Michael Rosen's first collection of poems, and I was the person who was fortunate enough to illustrate it. Michael Rosen has a wonderful power of recollection and he seems to know everything that happens in families between children (especially boys) and between them and their parents. One of the good things about his poems is that they tell you that it's good to have poems about how astonishing daffodils are, especially in large numbers, but that you can also have poems about doing the washing-up, and waiting for your mother to come back from hospital, and looking at old photographs, which are just as affecting.

Michael Rosen has done lots of other books with other illustrators. They are not all books of poems and I can't help mentioning two special favourites, both picture story books. One is *The Cardboard Box*, with pictures by Bob Graham (see page 26) and the other, is *Rover* with wild cheerful drawings by Neal Layton.

In the daytime I am Rob Roy and a tiger
In the daytime I am Marco Polo
       I chase bears in Bricket Wood
In the daytime I am the Tower of London
       nothing gets past me
       when it's my turn
       in Harrybo's hedge
In the daytime I am Henry the fifth and Ulysses
       and I tell stories
       that go on for a whole week
       if I want.
At night in the dark
       when I've shut the front room door
       I try and
       get up the stairs across the landing
       into bed and under the pillow
       without breathing once.

Heard it in the Playground
Allan Ahlberg
illustrated by Fritz Wegner

Allan Ahlberg's great collaboration was, for twenty years, with his artist wife Janet until her death in 1994; they were perfectly matched and everyone knows *Peepo!* and *The Jolly Postman* and many others. But Allan Ahlberg can probably write anything to do with children's books, at least to do with younger readers, and he has had many other successful collaborations. *Heard it in the Playground* is a collection of poems about school in which he is partnered by Fritz Wegner, whose drawings are both accurate and funny.

The Infants Do an Assembly about Time

The infants
Do an assembly
About Time.

It has the past,
The present
And the future in it;

The seasons,
A digital watch,

And a six-year-old
Little old lady.
She gets her six-year-old
Family up
And directs them
Through the twenty-four hours
Of the day:

Out of bed
And – shortly after –
Back into it.
(Life does not stand still
in infant assemblies.)

The whole thing
Lasts for fifteen minutes.
Next week (space permitting):
Space.

Three Has Gone
Jackie Kay

Like Michael Rosen, Jackie Kay seems to be able to
remember exactly what she felt when she was a child
– and writes it down in various voices which are both
like speech and, in urgency and emphasis, like poetry
at the same time.

REDDRICK

Today was Reddrick's birthday. Three already.
Only Reddrick no longer lives with me.
Reddrick lives at the end of the road with the
  Murrays.

I went along there to see if I could wish her the
  best.
To my great horror she was outside, covered in rust.
No saddle; holes of decay along her bars; trust,

for Reddrick, a thing of the past. When she was
  mine
there wasn't a single chip in her colour, red wine.
I could see my reflection in her hands.

'Reddrick,' I whispered through the Murrays' gate.
She didn't even raise her head. I was too late.
She didn't even manage a very weak or irate

'Hello, how have you been since I last saw you?'
Though I could tell she heard me through and
  through.
Right down to her one pedal. 'Reddrick. I love
  you.'

I went home and cried for an hour and a quarter.
Then I went downstairs to give my mother what for.
I started quite casually: 'You'll never guess who I
  saw
yesterday, Reddrick!' But my mum was hardly
  listening.
'Reddrick, my old bike, you gave to Anne Murray.
  Sickening
state she was in.' *Uh huh* my mum said, then back
  to reading.

I was so angry. I grabbed the paper and tore it in two.
'One day I just came home and Reddrick was gone.
  You
just gave her to the *poor Murrays* without asking. How

could you?' My mum was stunned. 'You didn't
  cycle any more, dear.'
'We didn't cycle. We talked.' I screamed and
  walked off. No fear.
She was wrong. Another birthday ruined. On to
  next year.

Figgie Hobbin
Charles Causley
illustrated by Gerald Rose

Figgie Hobbin is a kind of local pudding loved by Cornishmen. Charles Causley, who lives in Cornwall, is one of our most distinguished poets. His poems, both for adults and children, seem to have in them the sound and mysterious meaning of old spoken verse, whilst still being all about the present day.

MY YOUNG MAN'S A CORNISHMAN

My young man's a Cornishman
He lives in Camborne town,
I met him going up the hill
As I was coming down.

His eye is bright as Dolcoath tin,
His body as china clay,
His hair is dark as Werrington Wood
Upon St Thomas's Day.

He plays the rugby football game
On Saturday afternoon,
And we shall walk on Wilsey Down
Under the bouncing moon.

My young man's a Cornishman,
Won't leave me in the lurch,
And one day we shall married be
Up to Trura church*.

He's bought me a ring of Cornish gold,
A belt of copper made,
At Bodmin Fair for my wedding-dress
A purse of silver paid.

And I shall give him scalded cream
And starry-gazy pie+,
And make him a saffron cake for tea
And a pasty for by and by.

My young man's a Cornishman,
A proper young man is he,
And a Cornish man with a Cornish maid
Is how it belongs to be.

* Truro Cathedral
+ A starry-gazy is a fish pie, made of pilchards. The fish are cooked whole,
with the heads piercing the crust as though gazing up to the heavens.

The Mermaid's Purse
Ted Hughes

If it were not for Ted Hughes, I would not have been asked to put together this list of favourites. This is because in the last years of his life, when he was Poet Laureate, he responded to and promoted the idea of a Children's Laureate. He himself wrote many books for children: ones with crazy humour, like *Meet My Folks*, or strong and imaginative ones, like *The Iron Man* and *The Iron Woman*. What impressed me most, when I was younger, *were* those poems about animals and birds – like "Pike" and "The Hawk in the Rain" – where you could feel the harshness and energy of nature in the very way the words strained and crunched together. So it was a wonderful discovery to see this new collection of his verses; especially as they are about creatures that live in and around the sea. They are brought before us in terse and vivid portraits.

GULLS

Gulls are glanced from the lift
Of cliffing air
And left
Loitering in the descending drift,
Or tilt gradient and go
Down steep invisible clefts in the grain
Of air, blading against the blow,

Back-flip, wisp
Over the foam-galled green
Building seas, and they scissor
Tossed spray, shave sheen,
Wing-waltzing their shadows
Over the green hollows,

Or rise again in the wind's landward rush
And, hurdling the thundering bush
With the stone wall flung in their faces,
Repeat their graces.

Messages
Edited by Naomi Lewis

Messages doesn't come with illustrations or other added attractions; but once you get into it you discover that every poem is carefully chosen, and chosen by someone who knows poetry really well, is intimate with the way it works. Poems have messages, are messages, in all sorts of different ways. "The Wolf said to Francis" gives a message of the present day – but it isn't just propaganda. It's also a real imaginative experience, properly created. And there is a lot else to be found in *Messages*.

THE WOLF SAID TO FRANCIS
Naomi Lewis

The wolf said to Francis
'You have more sense than some.
I will not spoil the legend;
Call me, and I shall come.

But in the matter of taming
Should you not look more near?
Those howlings come from humans.
Their hatred is their fear.

We are an orderly people.
Though great our pain and need,
We do not kill for torture;
We do not hoard for greed.

94

But the victim has the vision –
A gift of sorts that's given
As some might say, by history
And you, perhaps, by heaven.

Tomorrow or soon after
(Count centuries for days)
I see (and you may also
If you will turn and gaze) –

How the sons of man have taken
A hundredfold their share.
But the child of God, the creature,
Can rest his head nowhere.

See, sky and ocean empty,
The earth scorched to the bone;
By poison, gun, starvation
The last free creature gone.
But the swollen tide of humans
Sweeps on and on and on.

No tree, no bird, no grassland
Only increasing man,
And the prisoned beasts he feeds on –
Was *this* the heavenly plan?'

Francis stood there silent.
Francis bowed his head.
Clearly passed before him
All that the wolf had said.

Francis looked at his brother
He looked at the forest floor.
The vision pierced his thinking,
And with it, something more
That humans are stony listeners.

The legend stands as before.

Old Possum's Book of Practical Cats
T.S. Eliot
illustrated by Edward Gorey

T.S. Eliot was probably the most famous poet in English of the twentieth century. He wrote one book of comic verse, which is *Practical Cats*. As well as being funny these poems are beautifully and carefully written, full of the skills of language and versification. Several people have illustrated the book, or parts of it, at one time and another; *my* favourite is the version by the American illustrator Edward Gorey.

from MACAVITY: THE MYSTERY CAT

Macavity's a Mystery Cat: he's called the Hidden Paw –
For he's the master criminal who can defy the Law.
He's the bafflement of Scotland Yard, the Flying Squad's
    despair:
For when they reach the scene of crime – *Macavity's not
    there!*

Macavity, Macavity, there's no one like Macavity,
He's broken every human law, he breaks the law of gravity.
His powers of levitation would make a fakir stare,
And when you reach the scene of crime – *Macavity's not there!*
You may seek him in the basement, you may look up in the
    air–
But I tell you once and once again, *Macavity's not there!*

Macavity's a ginger cat, he's very tall and thin;
You would know him if you saw him, for his eyes are sunken
    in.
His brow is deeply lined with thought, his head is highly
    domed;
His coat is dusty from neglect, whiskers are uncombed.
He sways his head from side to side, with movements like a
    snake;
And when you think he's half asleep, he's always wide awake.

A Shropshire Lad
A. E. Housman

This really is an experiment because I read these poems with interest when I was a teenager, but I don't know if any one of that age can read them in the same spirit now – after all, they are about farmers' boys a hundred years ago, and nowadays we mostly live in cities, and life is very different. However, there are still lads, and though now I suppose they mostly drink lager, they no doubt still get depressed. And these poems, although they are easily accessible, are well made – they almost seem to be cut out of some dense, heavy stone; so that if you return to them much later they are still there just as you left them.

ON WENLOCK EDGE

On Wenlock Edge the wood's in trouble;
 His forest fleece the Wrekin heaves;
The gale, it plies the saplings double,
 And thick on Severn snow the leaves.

'Twould blow like this through holt and hanger
 When Uricon the city stood:
'Tis the old wind in the old anger,
But then it threshed another wood.

Then, 'twas before my time, the Roman
 At yonder heaving hill would stare:
The blood that warms an English yeoman,
 The thoughts that hurt him, they were there.

There, like the wind through woods in riot,
 Through him the gale of life blew high;
The tree of man was never quiet:
 Then 'twas the Roman, now 'tis I.

The gale, it plies the saplings double,
 It blows so hard, 'twill soon be gone:
To-day the Roman and his trouble
 Are ashes under Uricon.

Nonsense Verse
Edward Lear

What I like about Edward Lear's nonsense limericks is that the form of the verse is always the same but the content is wild and unexpected; not to say sometimes alarming. I think I like the drawings even more. Because they were nonsense, and for children, and (to begin with) private, Lear could ignore the well-behaved manners that drawings were supposed to have in the nineteenth century when they appeared in public, and create something completely idiosyncratic, full of life and urgency and oddness.

There was an Old Man who said, 'Hush!
I perceive a young bird in this bush!'
When they said– 'Is it small?' He replied– 'Not at all!
It is four times as big as the bush!'

There was an Old Man with a beard,
Who sat on a horse when he reared;
But they said, 'Never mind! you will fall off behind,
You propitious Old Man with a beard!'

There was an Old Man, on whose nose,
Most birds of the air could repose;
But they all flew away, at the closing of day,
Which relieved that Old Man and his nose.

Lullabies, Lyrics and Gallows Songs
Christian Morgenstern, selected and illustrated by Lisbeth Zwerger

These are funny, odd and idiosyncratic poems very ingeniously translated from the German by Anthea Bell. They are sometimes rather like nonsense verses in the English tradition, but they have a special flavour of their own, enhanced by Lisbeth Zwerger's decorative, elegant, laid-back illustrations.

IN ANIMAL COSTUME

Palmstrom likes to imitate the animals
and keeps two young tailors busy
making nothing but animal costumes.

He loves to perch like a raven
on the very top branch of an oak tree,
watching the clouds sail by.

Or he likes to be a Saint Bernard,
shaggy head asleep on brave paws,
dreaming of people rescued from the snow.

Or he spins a string net in his garden,
dresses up, and sits all day
like a spider in its web.

Or he swims, a goggle-eyed carp,
around his fountain in his pool
and lets the children feed him.

Or he dangles in stork costume
from the basket of a balloon
and flies away to Egypt.

Books
for
Older
Readers

Alice Through the Looking Glass
Lewis Carroll

When I was small I didn't feel that Alice was somehow
quite what I wanted; it was only when I reached ado-
lescence that it became interesting to me, which is why
I have included it here. It's partly that Carroll remains
so straightfaced about it all and that Alice has what is
sometimes quite a frightening experience. (You can see
why the Surrealists liked it.) In addition to that there
is an economy and accuracy in the writing and an
unerring sense of the absurd that means that Alice is (as
people say of Shakespeare) 'full of quotations.'

"It's only the Red King snoring," said Tweedledee.

"Come and look at him," the brothers cried, and
they each took one of Alice's hands, and led her up
to where the King was sleeping.

"Isn't he a *lovely* sight?" said Tweedledum.

Alice couldn't say honestly that he was. He had a
tall red night-cap on, with a tassel, and he was lying
crumpled up into a sort of untidy heap, and snoring
loud - "fit to snore his head off!" as Tweedledum
remarked.

"I'm afraid he'll catch cold with lying on the damp
grass," said Alice, who was a very thoughtful little girl.

"He's dreaming now," said Tweedledee: "and what do
you think he's dreaming about?"

Alice said, "Nobody can guess that."

"Why, about *you!*" Tweedledee exclaimed, clapping his hands triumphantly. "And if he left off dreaming about *you*, where do you suppose you'd be?"

"Where I am now, of course," said Alice.

"Not you!" Tweedledee retorted contemptuously. "You'd be nowhere. Why, you're only a sort of thing in his dream!"

"If that there King was to wake," added Tweedledum, "you'd go out - bang - just like a candle!"

"I shouldn't!" Alice exclaimed indignantly. "Besides, if *I'm* only a sort of thing in his dream, what are *you*, I should like to know?"

"Ditto," said Tweedledum.

"Ditto, ditto!" cried Tweedledee.

He shouted this so loud that Alice couldn't help ssaying, "Hush! You'll be waking him, I'm afraid, if you make so much noise."

"Well, it's no use *your* talking about waking him," said Tweedledum, "when you're only one of the things in his dream. You know very well you're not real."

"I *am* real!" said Alice, and began to cry.

"You won't make yourself a bit realer by crying," Tweedledee remarked: "there's nothing to cry about."

"If I wasn't real," Alice said – half-laughing through her tears, it all seemed so ridiculous – "I shouldn't be able to cry."

"I hope you don't suppose those are real tears?" Tweedledum interrupted in a tone of great contempt.

Men at Arms
Terry Pratchett

Perhaps there is no point in mentioning Terry Pratchett because so many people have read his books already – except that I know that I didn't read them for a long time because I thought they were science-fiction, which I am not particularly interested in. But really, as Terry Pratchett explains, what they are is fantasy, and if they take place in a parallel universe (or rather a world following a course so erratic that it probably isn't parallel to anything) what happens is an amazing cooking-up of clichés, history, jokes, philosophical ideas, and a huge helping of the present day.

It was more than just a delicatessen. It was a sort of dwarf community centre and meeting place. The babble of voices stopped when Angua entered, bending almost double, but started up again with slightly more volume and a few laughs when Carrot followed. He waved cheerfully at the other customers.

Then he carefully removed two chairs. It was just possible to sit upright if you sat on the floor.

'Very... nice,' said Angua. 'Ethnic.'

'I come in here quite a lot,' said Carrot. 'The food's good and, of course, it pays to keep your ear to the ground.'

'That'd certainly be easy here,' said Angua, and laughed.

'Pardon?'

'Well, I mean, the ground is... so much... closer...'

She felt a pit opening wider with every word. The noise level had suddenly dropped again.

'Er,' said Carrot, staring fixedly at her. 'How can I put this? People are talking in Dwarfish... but they're listening in Human.'

'Sorry.'

Carrot smiled, and then nodded at the cook behind the counter and cleared his throat noisily.

'I think I might have a throat sweet somewhere – ' Angua began.

'I was ordering breakfast,' said Carrot.

'You know the menu off by heart?'

'Oh, yes. But it's written on the wall as well.'

Angua turned and looked again at what she'd thought were merely random scratches.

'It's Oggham,' said Carrot. 'An ancient and poetic runic script whose origins are lost in the mists of time but it's thought to have been invented even before the Gods.'

'Gosh. What does it say?'

Carrot really cleared his throat this time.

'SOSS, EGG, BEANS AND RAT 12P

SOSS, RAT AND FRIED SLICE 10P

CREAM-CHEESE RAT 9P

RAT AND BEANS 8P

RAT AND KETCHUP 7P

RAT 4P'

'Why does ketchup cost almost as much as a rat?' said Angua.

'Have you tried rat without ketchup?' said Carrot.

Huckleberry Finn
Mark Twain

I don't really know whether *Huckleberry Finn* is meant to be a book for adults or a book for children; I suspect that Mark Twain started writing it as a boy's book and it got so good that adults had to take it seriously. One reason for this was that Twain hit on the wonderful idea of Huck – a ragged, wild, uneducated boy who belonged to nobody – telling his story and his 'ignoramus' reaction to the fraudulence and brutality of much of the behaviour of 'civilised' adults. He takes up, for instance, with the escaped black slave, Jim (there was still slavery at the time the book was written), and rather than obey the law and give him away he finds he has to follow his natural instincts.

Huckleberry Finn has always had a great attraction for artists, and has been illustrated many times, often very strikingly. I was once lucky enough to be asked to produce a set of small drawings for an edition of it, so I couldn't resist using one of them here.

> The widow she cried over me, and called me a poor lost lamb, and she called me a lot of other names, too, but she never meant no harm by it. She put me in them new clothes again, and I couldn't do nothing but sweat and sweat, and feel all cramped up. Well, then, the old thing commenced again. The widow rung a bell for supper, and you had to come to time. When you got to the table you couldn't go right to eating, but you had to wait for the widow to tuck

down her head and grumble a little over the victuals, though there warn't really anything the matter with them. That is, nothing only everything was cooked by itself. In a barrel of odds and ends it is different; things get mixed up, and the juice kind of swaps around, and the things go better.

After supper she got out her book and learned me about Moses and the Bulrushers; and I was in a sweat to find out all about him; but by-and-by she let it out that Moses had been dead a considerable long time; so then I didn't care no more about him; because I don't take no stock in dead people.

Pretty soon I wanted to smoke, and asked the widow to let me. But she wouldn't. She said it was a mean practice and wasn't clean, and I must try not to do it any more. That is just the way with some people. They get down on a thing when they don't know nothing about it. Here she was a-bothering about Moses, which was no kin to her, and no use to anybody, being gone, you see, yet finding a power of fault with me for doing a thing that had some good in it. And she took snuff too; of course, that was all right, because she done it herself.

Tulku
Peter Dickinson

A former music-hall actress in search of rare plants; an amateur Chinese poet; the American son of a murdered missionary; all three together on a strange quest in Tibet in the late nineteenth century. It would be enough to imagine this situation, but Peter Dickinson writes about it with a convincing grasp of its seriousness and complexity that surpasses what one might expect in many an adult novel.

P'iu-Chun was on his feet and bowing stiffly from the waist, and so was Lung. Theodore, who had risen automatically (Father had always insisted he should stand even for the poorest peasant-woman, and had done so himself), copied them awkwardly.

"Honoured Princess, my poor cottage is yours," said P'iu Chun.

"The hospitality of the renowned What's-is-name makes any house a palace," fluted Mrs Jones when Lung had translated. "Got that out of a panto, when I was principal boy in Aladdin. Don't put that bit in."

Deftly Lung added a few courteous twiddles to account for the extra sentence. The exchange might have gone on for some time, but just as P'iu-Chun was bowing himself into a fresh compliment Mrs Jones gave a little cry and ran with fluttering steps towards the pictures on the wall.

"Why, these are lovely," she cried, still in her grand voice but somehow no longer acting. "That's *Rhododendron megeratum* – I've seen that in Nepal ... and *Paeonia lutea* – we all grow that now... what's this primula – I've never seen that? Lung, ask him where he got these perfectly adorable things, and who painted them."

"The Princess is a great lover of plants and admires the drawings," said Lung. "She names each plant in her own tongue. She asks who painted the pictures."

"My own poor hand made these scrawls," said P'iu-Chun, purring. Theodore fancied he could see a tear of pleasure in the corner of the dark little eyes. Mrs Jones understood what he was saying before Lung could translate, and once more darted across the room, seized his hand and patted it sofly. P'iu-Chun was obviously amazed by this behaiour, but too happy to resist.

"Oh, it wasn't you!" she cried. "Oh, how I wish I could draw like that. I have to paint, to make a record of what I've found, and I get them accurate – I mean you can see every petal and how it goes – but what I can't do is that... that..."

Despairing of words she gestured towards the drawings again with a single sweeping movement that exactly expressed the few flowing strokes with which P'iu-Chun had brought the flowers out of the paper.

Great Expectations
Charles Dickens

Someone gave me a copy of *Oliver Twist* to read when I was ten. I knew that it was a classic, which sounded difficult, and it *was* difficult, so I didn't try Dickens again until I left school. When I did I could hardly believe it was the same person – because this writer was gripping, vivid and tremendously funny. *Great Expectations* is a good place to start because it is best quality Dickens but only half the length of most of his books, though once you get the taste the long novels are not too long – it's just something to look forward to. Incidentally, television adaptations can be good or bad but they are never actually Dickens, which you can only get through the writing. The books are more real and more surreal than anything you see on the screen.

"Hold your noise!" cried a terrible voice, as a man started up from among the graves at the side of the church porch. "Keep still, you little devil, or I'll cut your throat!"

A fearful man, all in coarse grey, with a great iron on his leg. A man with no hat, and with broken shoes, and an old rag tied round his head. A man who had been soaked in water, and smothered in mud, and lamed by stones, and cut by flints, and stung by nettles, and torn by briars; who limped, and shivered, and glared and growled; and whose teeth chattered in his head as he seized me by the chin.

"Oh! Don't cut my throat, sir," I pleaded in terror.

114

"Pray don't do it, sir."

"Tell us your name!" said the man. "Quick!"

"Pip, sir."

"Once more," said the man, staring at me. "Give it mouth!"

"Pip. Pip, sir."

"Show us where you live," said the man. "Pint out the place!"

I pointed to where our village lay, on the flat in-shore among the alder-trees and pollards, a mile or more from the church.

The man, after looking at me for a moment, turned me upside down, and emptied my pockets. There was nothing in them but a piece of bread. When the church came to itself – for he was so sudden and strong that he made it go head over heels before me, and I saw the steeple under my feet – when the church came to itself, I say, I was seated on a high tombstone, trembling, while he ate the bread ravenously.

"You young dog," said the man, licking his lips, "what fat cheeks you ha' got."

I believe I was fat, though I was at that time undersized, for my years, and not strong.

"Darn Me if I couldn't eat 'em," said the man, with a threatening shake of his head, "and if I han't half a mind to't."

I earnestly expressed my hope that he wouldn't, and held tighter to the tombstone on which he had put me; partly, to keep myself upon it; partly, to keep myself from crying.

The Member of the Wedding
Carson McCullers

The Member of the Wedding is not told in the first person like *Huckleberry Finn*, but the author seems so close to F Jasmine, remembers so well the strangeness of ideas that you have about yourself when you are that age, and the endlessness of childhood afternoons, that it is almost like another version of her speaking. It's a world that is at once strange and familiar.

There was a watery kitchen mirror hanging above the sink. Frankie looked, but her eyes were grey as they always were. This summer she was grown so tall that she was almost a big freak, and her shoulders were narrow, her legs too long. She wore a pair of blue track shorts, a B.V.D. undervest, and she was barefooted. Her hair had been cut like a boy's, but it had not been cut for a long time and was now not even parted. The reflection in the glass was warped and crooked, but Frankie knew well what she looked like; she drew up her left shoulder and turned her head aside.

'Oh,' she said. 'They were the two prettiest people I ever saw. I just can't understand how it happened.'

'But what, Foolish?' said Berenice. 'Your brother come home with the girl he means to marry and took dinner today with you and your Daddy. They intend to marry at her home in Winter Hill this coming Sunday. You and your Daddy are going to the wedding. And that is the A and the Z of the matter. So whatever ails you?'

'I don't know,' said Frankie. 'I bet they have a good time every minute of the day.'

'Less us have a good time,' John Henry said.

'Us have a good time?' Frankie asked. "Us."
He was small to be six years old, but he had the largest knees that Frankie had ever seen, and on one of them there was alwys a scab of a bandage where he had fallen down and skinned himself. John Henry had a little screwed white face and he wore tiny gold-rimmed glasses. He watched all the cards very carefully, because he was in debt; he owed Berenice more than five million dollars.

'I bid one heart,' said Berenice.

'A spade,' said Frankie.

'I want to bid spades,' said John Henry. 'That's what I was going to bid.'

'Well, that's your tough luck. I bid them first.'

'Hush quarrelling,' said Berenice. 'To tell the truth, I don't think either one of you got such a grand hand to fight over the bid about. I bid two hearts.'

'I don't give a durn about it,' Frankie said. 'It is immaterial to me.'

Sheer Greed

When the publishers had heard enough of my whining and complaining about all the great people that I couldn't get into this book they said I could have twenty more as long as I stopped making a fuss about it. So here they are. Though I *can* think of others...

Lucy Cousins	The Maisy Books
Dr Heinrich Hoffman	Shock-headed Peter
Sara Fanelli	Wolf!
Bruce Ingham	When Martha's Away
John Burningham	Oi! Get Off Our Train
Raymond Briggs	The Snowman
Jill Murphy	Peace at Last
David McKee	Not Now Bernard
Colin McNaughton	Wish You Were Here (and I wasn't)

Babette Cole	Mummy Laid an Egg
Charlotte Voake	Alphabet Adventure
Tony Ross	Dr Xargle's Book Earthlings
Michael Foreman	War Boy
Walter de la Mare	Peacock Pie
Kenneth Grahame	The Wind in the Willows
Stephen Beisty	Cross Sections: Man O'War
R. L. Stevenson	Treasure Island
Rudyard Kipling	Kim
Jane Austen	Northanger Abbey
J. D. Salinger	The Catcher in the Rye

P.S. — Shakespeare

Shakespeare hasn't been entirely left out of this book, because he is an important character in *King of Shadows*; but as he is the best and most famous English writer, and one of my favourites, I thought there should be some other mention of him. The problem is that reading him is not really the way to start off, and for two reasons. One is the difficulty of the language – some of it is complicated, and there are words we've lost the use of. The other is that while you are reading you have to imagine the action; and it takes some practice to do that. The best thing is to see good productions, because they carry you along even if you don't follow all the words; or to take part in a production. That way you learn the words - the sound of them gets stamped into your brain so that you never really forget them – and you get a grasp of the sense of the play. And it isn't so difficult; I remember, years ago, doing a shortened version of *Julius Caesar* with a class of eleven-year-olds.

On the day of the performance they all knew their lines perfectly, and we had a very good assassination with lots of blood. It's wonderful how it all comes to life.

You can also get something from cinema. *Shakespeare in Love* gives you some idea of the stage and acting (though I imagine Shakespeare must have been a more interesting person than he appears to be in the film). There are various film versions of the plays, of which the most interesting recent one is Baz Luhrmann's *Romeo and Juliet*; which is updated, outrageously but wittily, to a rather decadent California-type place called Verona Beach. All the words are by Shakespeare, and the film gives a much more vivid account of the play than some other more respectful stage versions have done. You understand what those people are like; and it's exciting and dangerous. Anyway, whichever way you get into Shakespeare, it's worth it when you get there.

Your Booklist

Your Booklist

Booklist

The Tale of Two Bad Mice
Beatrix Potter published by Frederick Warne
& Co.

The Madeline Books
Ludwig Bemelmans published by Scholastic
Ltd

What Can You Do With a Shoe?
Beatrice Schenk De Regniers, illustrated by
Maurice Sendak, published by Simon &
Schuster Ltd

Where the Wild Things Are
Maurice Sendak, published by Jonathan Cape

Doctor De Soto
William Steig, published by Andersen Press

Follow My Leader
Emma Chichester Clark, published by
Andersen Press

More!
Emma Chichester Clark, published by
Andersen Press

Little Babaji
Helen Bannerman, illustrated by Fred
Marcellino, published by Ragged Bear

Crusher is Coming
Bob Graham, published by Collins

Queenie the Bantam
Bob Graham, published by Walker Books Ltd

The Necessary Cat
Nicola Bayley, published by Walker Books Ltd

The Sea-Thing Child
Russell Hoban, illustrated by Patrick Benson,
published by Walker Books Ltd

*How Tom Beat Captain Najork
and his Hired Sportsmen*
Russell Hoban, illustrated by Quentin Blake,
published by Jonathan Cape

Clever Bill
William Nicholson, published by
Scholastic Ltd

Le Carnet d'Albert
Bruno Heitz, published by Circonflexe,
France

Snow-white
Josephine Poole, illustrated by Angela Barrett,
published by Hutchinson

Rose Blanche
Roberto Innocenti, text by Ian McEwan,
published by Jonathan Cape

The Lost Giants
François Place, published by Pavilion Books

A Ruined House
Mick Manning, published by Walker Books
Ltd

The Eighteenth Emergency
Betsy Byars, published by Red Fox

Arabel and Mortimer
Joan Aiken, illustrated by Quentin Blake,
published by Jonathan Cape

The Winter Sleepwalker
Joan Aiken, illustrated by Quentin Blake,
published by Jonathan Cape

Underrunners
Margaret Mahy, published by Penguin Books
Ltd

*The Great Piratical Rumbustification and The
Librarian and the Robbers*
Margaret Mahy, published by Puffin Books

Uncle Stories
J.P. Martin, illustrated by Quentin Blake,
published by Red Fox

Featherbrains
John Yeoman, illustrated by Quentin Blake,
published by Penguin Books Ltd

The Heron and the Crane
John Yeoman, illustrated by Quentin Blake,
published by Penguin Books Ltd

Emil and the Detectives
Erich Kästner, illustrated by Walter Trier,
published by Jonathan Cape

The Granny Project
Anne Fine, published by Scholastic Ltd

The Indian in the Cupboard
Lynne Reid Banks, published by J M Dent

Charlotte's Web
E B White, published by Puffin Books

Stuart Little
E B White, illustrated by Garth Williams,
published by Puffin Books

The Box of Delights and *The Midnight Folk*,
John Masefield, illustrated by Quentin Blake,
published by Heinemann

His Dark Materials (Trilogy)
Philip Pullman, published by Scholastic Ltd

Esio Trot
Roald Dahl, illustrated by Quentin Blake,
published by Jonathan Cape

The Twits
Roald Dahl, illustrated by Quentin Blake,
published by Jonathan Cape

The BFG
Roald Dahl, illustrated by Quentin Blake,
published by Jonathan Cape

Great Northern?
Arthur Ransome, published by Red Fox

King of Shadows
Susan Cooper, published by The Bodley Head

The Lost World
Sir Arthur Conan Doyle, published by
Penguin Books Ltd

Kensuke's Kingdom
Michael Morpurgo, published by Egmont

Lord of the Flies
William Golding, published by Faber & Faber
Ltd

Mind Your Own Business
Michael Rosen, illustrated by Quentin Blake,
published by Scholastic Ltd

Peepo! and *The Jolly Postman*
Janet and Allan Ahlberg, published by Penguin
Books Ltd

Heard it in the Playground
Allan Ahlberg, illustrated by Fritz Wegner,
published by Penguin Books Ltd

Three Has Gone
Jackie Kay, published by Blackie

Figgie Hobbin
Charles Causley, illustrated by Gerald Rose,
published by Macmillan

The Mermaid's Purse
Ted Hughes, published by Faber & Faber Ltd

Messages
Edited by Naomi Lewis, published by Faber
& Faber Ltd

Old Possum's Book of Practical Cats
T.S. Eliot, illustrated by Edward Gorey,
published by Faber & Faber Ltd

Nonsense Ryhmes
Edward Lear, published by Faber & Faber Ltd

Lullabies, Lyrics and Gallows Songs
Christan Morgenstern, chosen and illustrated
by Lisbeth Zwerger, published by North
South Books

Men at Arms
Terry Pratchett, published by Doubleday

Tulku
Peter Dickinson, published by Penguin Books
Ltd

The Maisy Books
Lucy Cousins, published by Walker Books Ltd

Wolf
Sara Fanelli, published by Heinemann

When Martha's Away
Bruce Ingham, published by Methuen

Oi! Get Off Our Train
John Burningham, published by Jonathan
Cape

The Snowman
Raymond Briggs, published by Puffin Books

Peace at Last
Jill Murphy, published by Macmillan

Not Now Bernard
David McKee, published by Red Fox

Wish You Were Here (and I wasn't)
Colin Mc Naughton, published by Walker
Books Ltd

Mummy Laid an Egg
Babette Cole, published by Jonathan Cape

Alphabet Adventure
Charlotte Voake, published by Jonathan Cape

Dr Xargle's Book of Earthlings
Jean Willis illustrated by Tony Ross,
published by Red Fox

War Boy
Michael Foreman, published by Pavilion

Peacock Pie
Walter de la Mare, published by Faber &
Faber Ltd

Cross Sections: Man O' War
Stephen Beisty, published byDorling
Kindersley

The Catcher in the Rye
J.D. Salinger, published by Penguin Books Ltd

The following books can be obtained in
various editions:

Northanger Abbey
Jane Austen

Alice Through the Looking Glass
Lewis Carroll

Robinson Crusoe
Daniel Defoe

*A Christmas Carol, Oliver Twist,
Great Expectations*
Charles Dickens

Wind in the Willows
Kenneth Grahame

Shock-headed Peter
Dr Heinrich Hoffman

A Shropshire Lad
A.E. Housman

Five Children and It
E Nesbit,

Treasure Island
R.L. Stevenson,

Huckleberry Finn
Mark Twain

ACKNOWLEDGEMENTS

The publishers wish to thank the following for permission to reproduce previously published material: Andersen Press for the extracts from *Dr De Soto* by William Steig and *More!* by Emma Chichester Clark; The Curtis Brown Ltd, London, on behalf of Atrium Verlag AG, Zurich. Copyright Atrium Verlag AG for the extract from *Emil and the Detectives* by Erich Kästner, illustrated by Walter Trier, published by Jonathan Cape; The Bodley Head and Viking Penguin, a division of Penguin Putnam Inc. for the extract from *The Eighteenth Emergency* by Betsy Byars, © 1973, illustrated by Quentin Blake; and The Bodley Head and Margaret K. McElderry Books, an imprint of Simon & Schuster Children's Publishing Division for the extract from *King of Shadows* by Susan Cooper ©1999; Jonathan Cape for the extracts from *Great Northern?* by Arthur Ransome, *Uncle and the Treacle Trouble* by J.P. Martin, illustrated by Quentin Blake and *The Winter Sleepwalker* by Joan Aiken, illustrated by Quentin Blake; Circonflexe for the extract from *Le Carnet d'Albert*, Circonflexe © 1994; Copyright © 1996 The Sir Arthur Conan Doyle Copyright Holders. Reprinted by kind permission of Jonathan Clowes Ltd., London, on behalf of Andrea Plunket, Administrator of the Sir Arthur Conan Doyle Copyrights; J. M. Dent for the extract from; *The Indian In the Cupboard*, by Lynne Reid Banks; Egmont Children's Books Ltd for the extracts from *The Granny Project* by Anne Fine and *Clever Bill* by William Nicholson; Faber & Faber Ltd for "Gulls" from *The Mermaid's Purse* by Ted Hughes, the extract from "Macavity; the Mystery Cat" from *Old Possum's Book of Practical Cats* by T. S. Eliot, illustrated by Edward Gorey and the extract from *Rumplestiltskin and Other Grimm Tales* by Carol Ann Duffy, illustrated by Markéta Prachatická; David Higham Associates for the extracts from *Esio Trot* by Roald Dahl, illustrated by Quentin Blake, published by Jonathan Cape, *Kensuke's Kingdom*, by Michael Morpurgo, published by Egmont Children's Books Ltd and *Figgie Hobbin* by Charles Causley, illustrated by Gerald Rose, published by Macmillan; Hutchinson for the extract from *Rose Blanche* by Ian McEwan, illustrated by Roberto Innocenti and *Snow-white*, by Josephine Poole, illustrated by Angela Barrett; Naomi Lewis for "The Wolf said to Francis" from *Messages* published by Faber & Faber Ltd; ; Pavilion Books for the extract from *The Last Giants* by François Place; Penguin Books Ltd for "The Infants Do an Assembly about Time" from *Heard It In the Playground* by Allan Ahlberg, illustrated by Fritz Wegner, *Featherbrains* by John Yeoman, illustrated by Quentin Blake, *Stuart Little* by E.B. White and *Underrunners* by Margaret Mahy; Laurence Pollinger Ltd for the extract from *The Member of the Wedding* by Carson McCullers,. published by Penguin Books Ltd; Ragged Bear for the extract from *The Story of Little Babaji* by Helen Bannerman, illustrated by Fred Marcellino; Scholastic Ltd for the extracts from *Little Tim and the Brave Sea Captain* by Edward Ardizzone, *Madeline* by Ludwig Bemelmans, *Mind your Own Business* by Michael Rosen and *Northern Lights*, by Philip Pullman; Simon & Schuster Ltd for the extract from *What Can You Do With A Shoe?* by Beatrice Schenk de Regniers, illustrated by Maurice Sendak; The Society of Authors as the Literary Representative of the Estate of A.E. Housman for "On Wenlock Edge"; A. P. Watt on behalf of Peter Dickinson for the extract from *Tulku* by Peter Dickinson, published by Penguin Books Ltd. The Extract from Three Has Gone by Jackie Kay is reprinted by permission of the Peters Fraser & Dunlop Group Ltd; *The Necessary Cat*,© 1998 Nicola Bayley, *Queenie the Bantam*,© 1997 Bob Graham, *A Ruined House*,© 1994 Mick Manning and *The Sea-Thing Child*, text© 1972, 1999 Russell Hoban, illustrations© 1999 Patrick Benson. Reproduced by permission of the publisher Walker Books Ltd, London; Illustration and extract from *The Tale of Two Bad Mice*, by Beatrix Potter. Copyright© Frederick Warne & Co., 1904, 1987. Reproduced by kind permission of Frederick Warne & Co. *Lullabies, Lyrics and Gallow Songs* of Christian Morgenstern, selected and illustrated by Lisbeth Zwerger,© 1992/1995 North South Books, an imprint of Nord-Sud Verlag AG, Zurich/Switzerland; *Men At Arms*:© Terry and Lyn Pratchett. Extracted from *Men and Arms* by Terry Pratchett, published by Doubleday, a division of Transworld Publishers. All rights reserved. Every effort has been made to trace the holders of copyright material in this book. If any query should arise it should be addressed to the publishers.